A Lion for a Night

Of Monsters and Messes Book #3

Written By: RM Morrissey

Illustrated By: Ila Taylor Bologni

First Published 2023 by RM Morrissey

ISBN: 9798387524080

Copyright © RM Morrissey, 2023

A CIP catalogue record for this book is available from the British Library.

This book belongs to:

_____

Want more? Check out the last page for a link to a free ebook. For other free content and to be updated on future book releases, follow me on Instagram!

@rmorrisseybooks

Now, most people know all about monsters from under the bed. They might not want to admit it, but deep down, they all know they're there.

We curl our toes under the blankets hoping we don't get snatched. We wonder where on Earth our missing socks have gone. And we hear those noises creeping in the night when the darkness blinds our eyes.

But a little-known fact is that monsters can only show up at midnight. Not a second before and not a second after, for the portal only opens once every night at exactly the stroke of midnight.

Now, Jenkins, he believed in monsters under the bed, just like you should! They had to exist. His mum said his dirty socks and underwear hadn't vanished but were buried in the mess of his room.

Jenkins, he knew better ... the monsters, they were eating his clothes! That's how he knew they existed. It couldn't possibly be because he was messy!

Jenkins was a super lazy kid, and sleep was his favourite thing. Always, before bed, he'd brush his teeth and shower because, despite being messy, being dirty was something that just wouldn't do.

He'd avoid the mess in his room, find his sloth onesie in his closet and slink into bed to dream of food - his second favourite thing!
He'd sleep through the whole night - dead to the world.

Except when he didn't. Tonight, something was different.
Tonight, as the clock struck midnight, Jenkins heard a
sound. A soft, scurrying pitter-patter across the floor.

"Whah! What was that?!"

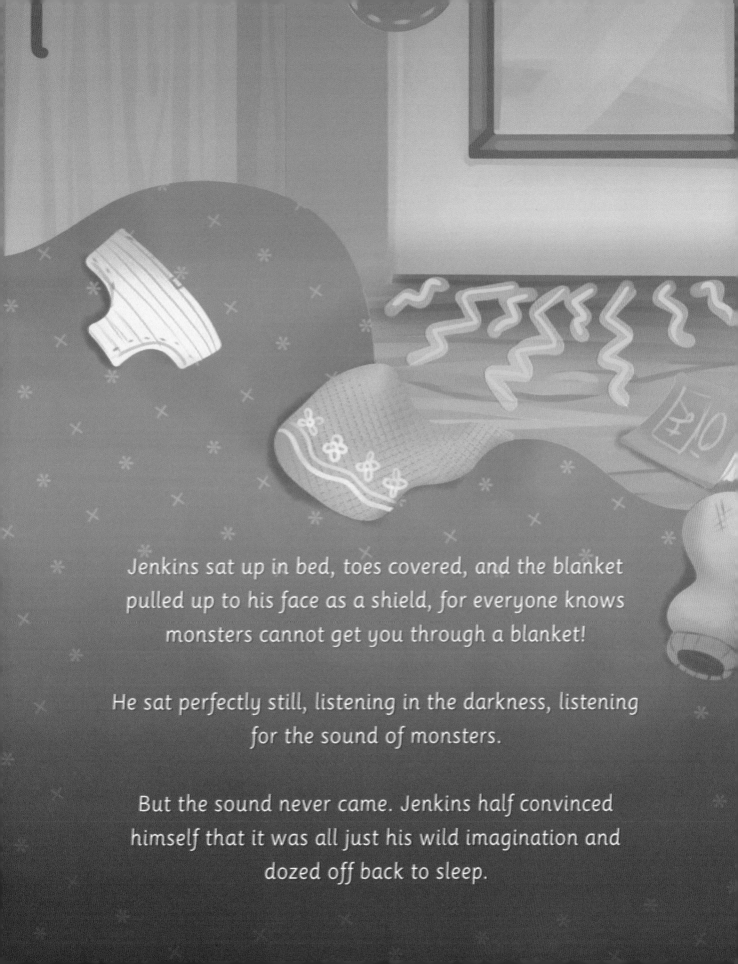

Jenkins sat up in bed, toes covered, and the blanket
pulled up to his face as a shield, for everyone knows
monsters cannot get you through a blanket!

He sat perfectly still, listening in the darkness, listening
for the sound of monsters.

But the sound never came. Jenkins half convinced
himself that it was all just his wild imagination and
dozed off back to sleep.

When Jenkins heard it again, it could have been minutes or hours - time all feels the same in the pitch black.

The sound! A scratchy, scritchy noise of claws across the floorboards.

"No … no, no, no!" Jenkins shook his head. "The monsters just want your dirty socks and underwear. Don't worry. You're safe under your covers."

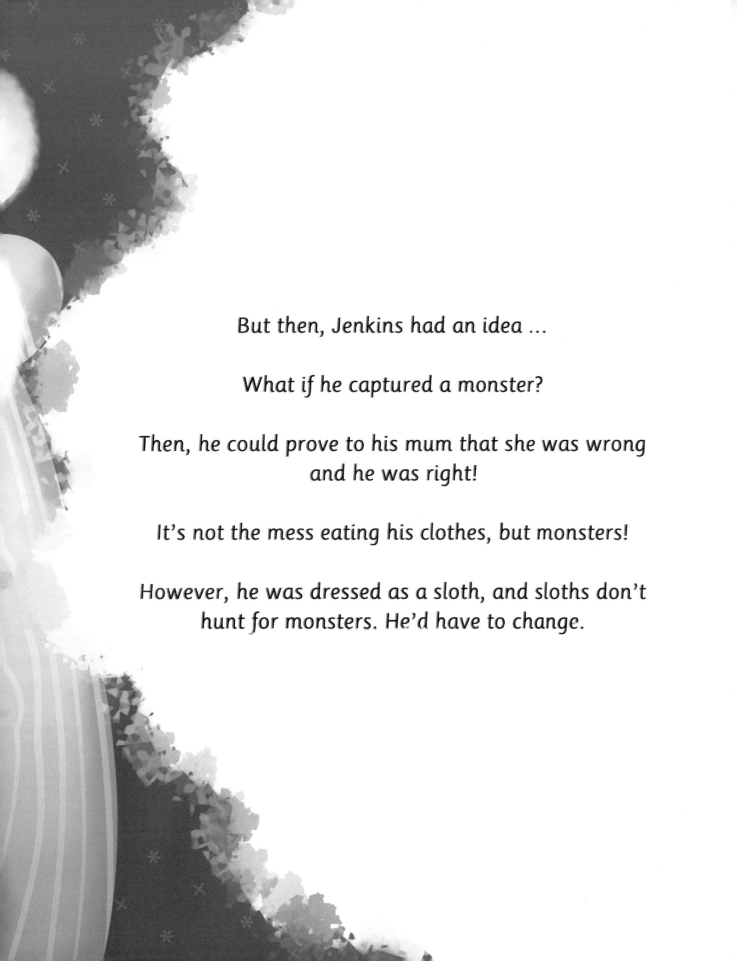

But then, Jenkins had an idea ...

What if he captured a monster?

Then, he could prove to his mum that she was wrong
and he was right!

It's not the mess eating his clothes, but monsters!

However, he was dressed as a sloth, and sloths don't
hunt for monsters. He'd have to change.

He jumped from his bed to his closet, careful no monster
could get his toes. And there, he found his lion onesie,
complete with paws for protection!

"As brave as a lion! Ha!
Time to catch me, a sock-stealing monster!"

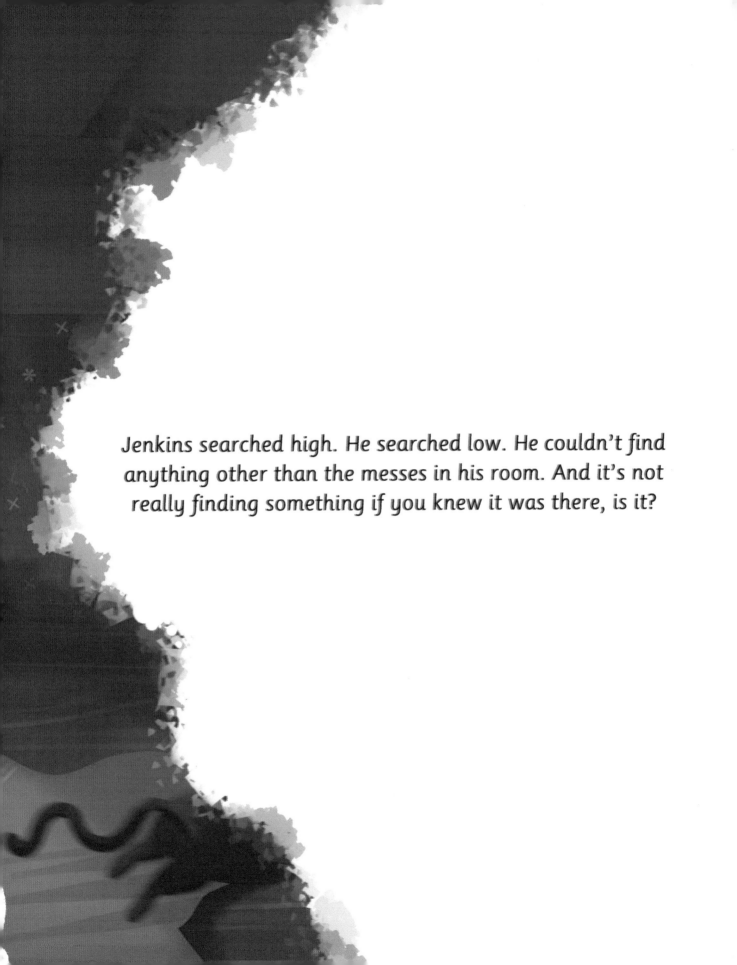

Jenkins searched high. He searched low. He couldn't find anything other than the messes in his room. And it's not really finding something if you knew it was there, is it?

He searched in his drawers, pulling out all of his clean clothes.

"Hmm, that sneaky, sock-stealing monster isn't in my drawers …"

He searched on his desk, rummaging through all of his papers
and homework, tossing them to the floor.

"Blah, that sneaky, sock-stealing monster isn't on my desk ..."

He even searched at the bottom of his laundry basket, tossing all his dirty clothes here, there and everywhere.

"Hmph, that sneaky, sock-stealing monster isn't in my laundry, either."

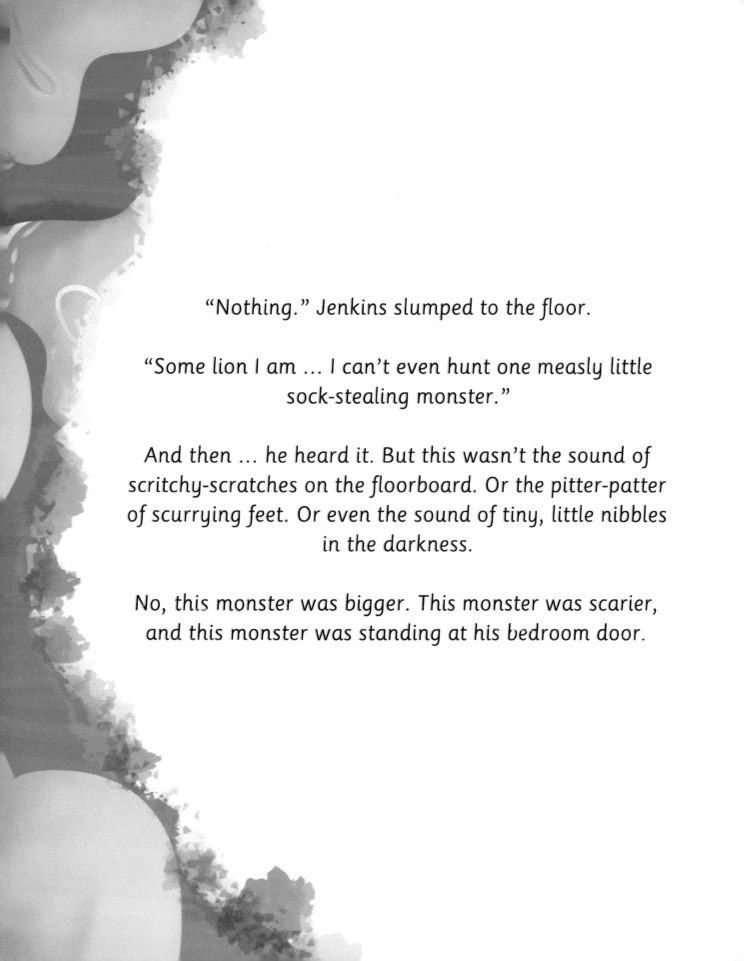

"Nothing." Jenkins slumped to the floor.

"Some lion I am ... I can't even hunt one measly little sock-stealing monster."

And then ... he heard it. But this wasn't the sound of scritchy-scratches on the floorboard. Or the pitter-patter of scurrying feet. Or even the sound of tiny, little nibbles in the darkness.

No, this monster was bigger. This monster was scarier, and this monster was standing at his bedroom door.

"Jenkins! What on Earth are you doing, and what and why? No, how is it possible for your room to be even messier than normal?!"

"But Mum! There's a monster! I'm hunting it. I need to –"

"Enough, Jenkins. It's the middle of the night. I have no time for your monsters or messes. Go to bed, and you will clean this up in the morning."

"B-b-bu–"

"No buts. Bed. Now."

Jenkins slouched his shoulders, and sighed as he walked back to his closet. He put on his sloth onesie. And, like his usual lazy self, he crawled into bed.

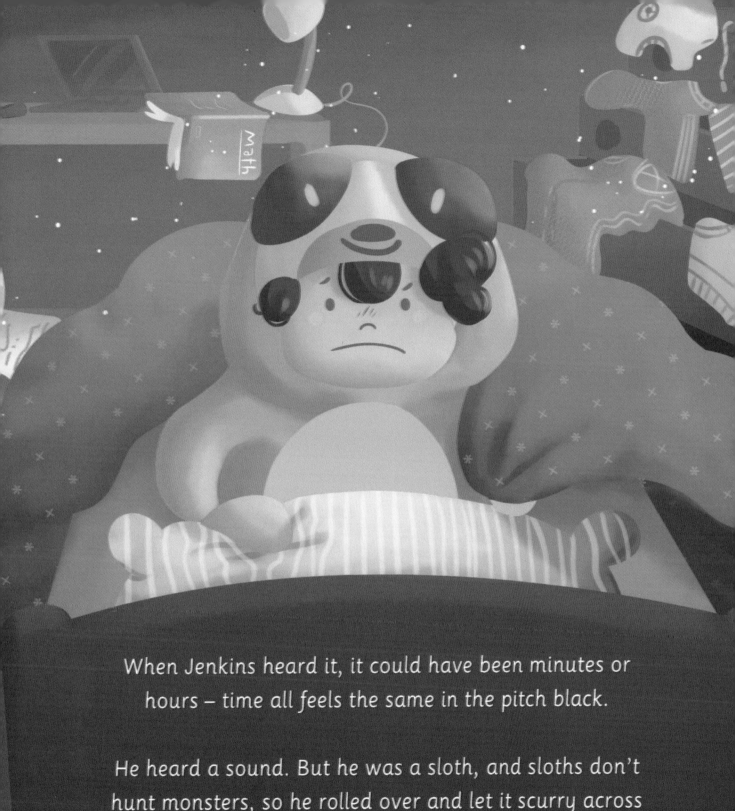

When Jenkins heard it, it could have been minutes or hours – time all feels the same in the pitch black.

He heard a sound. But he was a sloth, and sloths don't hunt monsters, so he rolled over and let it scurry across the floor with its scritchy-scratchy feet, crawl under his door and pitter-patter to who knows where ...

ACKNOWLEDGMENTS

Thank you to all of the children who have
given me excellent feedback on the many, many
many versions of this book. It has been a wonderful
experience working with you, listening to your likes
and dislikes.

Children truly make excellent editors!

If you enjoyed reading the book, consider
following me on Instagram for links to
free content and to be updated
on future book releases.

@rmorrisseybooks